Bright
≡Summaries.com

The Unknown Masterpiece

BY HONORÉ DE BALZAC

The Unknown Masterpiece

by Honoré de Balzac

HONORÉ DE BALZAC   5

French Writer   5

THE UNKNOWN MASTERPIECE   6

A Reflection on the Powers of Art   6

SUMMARY   7

Part 1 – Gillette   7
Part Two – Catherine Lescault   9

CHARACTER STUDY   11

Frenhofer   11
Nicolas Poussin   12
Gillette   13
Porbus   14

KEYS TO READING   16

A Two-Faceted Story   16
A Romantic Conception of Art   21
Significant Mythological References   23
The Question of *Mimesis*   24
A Legacy in the Arts   25

AVENUES FOR FEFLECTION   28

A Few Questions for Further Reflection…   28

TO GO FURTHER   30

Reference Edition   30
Baseline Study   30
Adaptation   30

HONORÉ DE BALZAC

FRENCH WRITER

- **Born in 1799 in Tours (Indre-et-Loire)**
- **Died in 1850 in Paris**
- **Some of his works:**
  - *Les Chouans* (1829), novel
  - *Eugénie Grandet* (1833), novel
  - *Le Père Goriot* (1835), novel

Honoré de Balzac is one of the major French writers of the 19th century. As a young man, he opened the doors of aristocratic Parisian circles, which he never stopped frequenting. However, disastrous business ventures and an excessive lifestyle soon ruined him: literary writing, practised with passion and assiduity, became the only way for him to pay off his debts.

Ambitious, he set about writing a monumental work, *La Comédie humaine*, which includes more than 90 novels. His aim was to draw up an exhaustive portrait of the society of his time, in order to "compete with the État-Civil" (DE BALZAC H. *OEuvres complètes*, tome I, Paris, Alexandre Houssiaux, 1855, p. 22).

Balzac is considered one of the fathers of the modern realistic novel.

THE UNKNOWN MASTERPIECE

A REFLECTION ON THE POWERS OF ART

- **Genre:** short story

- **Reference edition:** *Le Chef-d'œuvre inconnu* suivi de *La Leçon de violon*, Paris, Le Livre de Poche, coll. « Les classiques d'aujourd'hui », 2002.

- **1st edition:** 1831

- **Themes:** art, painting, *mimesis*, mythology, perfection, madness

The Unknown Masterpiece is a short story that first appeared in 1831 under the title *Maître Frenhofer* in the magazine *L'Artiste*, before being included in a subset of *La Comédie humaine*: the *Études philosophiques*.

The plot is set in the 17th century and focuses on the character of Frenhofer, a painter who has the ambition to paint a perfect portrait of a woman. The novella thus offers a reflection on the powers of art and on the condition of the painter.

This short story by Balzac had a certain posterity and was a source of inspiration for writers and painters alike.

SUMMARY

PART 1 – GILLETTE

The story takes place in Paris in 1612. A young man visits the home of François Porbus (Frans Pourbus the Younger, Flemish painter, 1569-1622), the former painter of Henri IV (King of France and Navarre, 1553-1610), who was dismissed by Marie de Medici (Queen of France, 1573-1642), who preferred Rubens (Flemish painter, 1577-1640) to him. The visitor, who also happens to be an artist, is impressed by the idea of this meeting and, out of shyness, does not dare to go up to Porbus' studio. Eventually an old man joins him on the stairs and knocks on the door, after which both are ushered by Porbus into a room cluttered with painting equipment.

The old man then launches into a long commentary on a painting by Porbus of St Mary the Egyptian (Christian penitent, c. 345-c. 422). Although the painting seemed to him to be perfectly executed from a technical point of view, he criticised it for not giving a strong enough impression of reality. For him, the woman Porbus painted does not seem sufficiently alive: "You have the appearance of life, but you do not express its overflowing fullness." (p. 45).

The young man reacts by praising Porbus' painting. He introduces himself: his name is Nicolas Poussin (French painter, 1594-1665) and he is a trainee artist. The old man then asks Porbus for brushes and colours and, with a few strokes of paint, he succeeds in transforming the representation of Mary the Egyptian, giving it a real breath of life. Despite this, he finds that it is still not as good as his masterpiece, *La Belle Noiseuse*.

The old painter – whose name, we learn from Porbus, is Frenhofer – then invites the two men to his house for dinner, where some magnificent paintings are gathered. Poussin is captivated by their beauty. Porbus tells Frenhofer that he wants to see *La Belle Noiseuse*, the famous painting of a woman the old man has named Catherine Lescault, which he has been working on for ten years. Frenhofer replies that he still has to perfect it, then explains how he has worked on it and admits that despite all the mistakes he has been able to avoid, he doubts his work. He wonders if he will ever find a perfect woman to use as a model.

The other two painters move away from Frenhofer, who is lost in thought. Poussin wants to go to the old man's studio, but Porbus tells him that no one is allowed in. The neophyte, who does not understand this, is determined to enter the place where Frenhofer creates his paintings.

Back at the hotel where he is staying, he asks Gillette, his beautiful companion, if she would agree to pose for a man other than him, which would allow him to become a great painter. Poussin hopes that in exchange for the woman he loves, Frenhofer will agree to show him his masterpiece, which holds the secrets of pictorial art. At first Gillette refuses, because she feels that such an action would make her unworthy of being loved by Poussin and that he would consequently abandon her. Finally, she agrees on condition that he stays behind the door of the room in which she is to be modelled and that he kills the painter if she ever screams. The girl, who feels that Poussin is obsessed with art and no longer loves her, immediately regrets the commitment she has made.

PART TWO – CATHERINE LESCAULT

Three months after the three men met, Porbus visits Frenhofer, who is more discouraged than ever. The old painter thought he had finally finished his painting, but some details still need to be reworked. He intends to travel to Turkey, Greece and Asia to find new female models. Porbus tells him that he could spare him the trip, as Poussin's companion is a physically perfect woman and is willing to pose for him if, in exchange, he and Poussin are allowed to see his work. Like a possessive lover, the old man categorically refuses to expose his "wife" (p. 65) to the gaze of other men.

While Porbus, surprised by the violence with which Frenhofer reacts, is about to give up, Poussin and Gillette arrive at the old man's house. The old man observes the young girl attentively and undresses her with his eyes. Poussin is jealous and wants to return home with his companion, but Frenhofer finally agrees to the deal. The young painter then threatens to kill him if he does anything to Gillette.

After some time, Frenhofer opens the door to his studio and invites Porbus and Poussin to enter. They admire the paintings there, which Frenhofer calls "mistakes" (p. 72). He assures them that his latest work is perfect, that the woman he has painted is truer than life. But when Porbus and Poussin look at the canvas, they see nothing more than a juxtaposition of layers of colour. In the middle of this "wall of paint" (p. 74), only a foot, which seems to be real, emerges. At first Poussin thinks that the old man is making fun of them, but then realises that he is sincere: Frenhofer is delirious and is convinced that the other two painters really do see the female body he is describing.

Poussin tells Porbus that sooner or later Frenhofer will realise that nothing is represented on his canvas. The old man hears this remark and gets angry. He then asks Porbus if he has spoiled his painting. Porbus, who does not know what to say, points to his canvas and says, "Look!" (p. 76). Frenhofer realises that there is no female figure in the painting. He is desperate, weeps and calls himself crazy. But immediately afterwards he accuses the two artists of being envious and of planning to steal his masterpiece.

Poussin suddenly hears Gillette crying. She would like her young companion, whom she finds contemptuous, to kill her. The old man is very suspicious and throws them all out. The next day, Porbus wants to see Frenhofer again, but he learns that he has died after burning all his paintings to ashes.

CHARACTER STUDY

FRENHOFER

A wealthy old man, Frenhofer was an exceptional artist. He claims to have been the only pupil of the Flemish painter Mabuse (ca. 1478-1532). He has a thorough knowledge of painting, both from a technical and art historical point of view. He does not hesitate to share his knowledge and willingly gives advice to younger artists.

He is a man of mystery: no one has ever had the opportunity to enter his studio to admire his work, and he has never had a pupil to whom he could confide the secrets of his technique. For him, painting is a truly sacred practice.

His big project is to create a painting of a woman who looks like she is real. For years Frenhofer has dedicated his life to this painting. Time and again, he thinks he has finally finished it, but each time he realises that some of the details do not reach the perfection he is looking for.

The painter's obsession with his masterpiece, which he calls his Catherine Lescault, gradually drives him into madness. The text provides several clues to his faltering mental health:

- the narrator calls him "a singular character who talks so madly" (p. 47);

- Porbus says that he is "as mad as he is a painter" (p. 60);

- the old man behaves as if the woman he is painting is really his wife. Thus, for him to show her to other men is an act of prostitution. When he expresses all the love he feels for her figure, the narrator asks: "Was Frenhofer reasonable or mad?"

In the end, Porbus' and Poussin's reactions to his painting make him realise how delirious he is. He cannot bear this harsh return to reality, and death becomes his only escape.

NICOLAS POUSSIN

Balzac chose to insert a real painter into his fiction. Nicolas Poussin is one of the great French masters of pictorial classicism. In the novella, the author presents him as a young, still unknown beginner. He has only recently arrived in Paris and lives in poverty. This does not prevent him from being talented: Frenhofer compliments him when he skilfully copies Porbus' painting.

The young man is torn between two seemingly incompatible passions. On the one hand, he longs to become a great painter. He discovers Frenhofer on his way to Porbus's house and wants to learn the secrets of art, so he tries to convince the old man to let him into his studio. On the other hand, he is in love with Gillette, his lover: the fact that she poses for Frenhofer makes him sad, gloomy and remorseful. He is overcome with jealousy, which directly echoes the old painter's attitude towards his work (both are prepared to kill for their beloved).

The love of art, however, seems to be stronger than anything else:

- When Gillette refuses his offer to pose for another man, he seems at first to accept her choice ("I was mistaken, my vocation is to love you. I am not a painter, I am in love," p. 63). But immediately afterwards he tries to convince her again, explaining that Frenhofer is just an old man;

- Gillette realises the passion with which her lover looks at a painting by Frenhofer, which he has mistaken for a Giorgione (Venetian painter, 1477-1510): "He never looked at me like that" (p. 71), she says;

- When he enters Frenhofer's studio and discovers pictorial wonders, he completely forgets about his companion, until her sobs catch his attention.

GILLETTE

Gillette is Poussin's lover, with whom she is deeply in love. The narrator describes her as obedient and cheerful, but it is her physical beauty that characterises her above all. She is at the heart of the agreement between Frenhofer and the other two painters, precisely because she has a perfect body.

Dignified, she does not at first agree to reveal her nakedness to a stranger. But Gillette is "one of those noble and generous souls who come to suffer near a great man" (p. 61). She is therefore prepared to sacrifice herself for Poussin's career, even though she is convinced that their love will not stand the test. Deep down, she is disappointed by her companion's attitude, which makes her a bargaining chip ("She already thought she loved the painter less by suspecting him to be less estimable," p. 64).

The bad feeling she has just before entering Frenhofer's house is the author's way of announcing the tragic outcome of the story. After having served as a model, she seems to be devastated and, full of rage, claims to hate Poussin.

PORBUS

Porbus is the second real painter to be a character in the novel: Frans Pourbus the Younger is a Flemish painter who worked for the French court. Among his most important works is the portrait of the French King Henry IV, which Balzac mentions in *The Unknown Masterpiece*.

He is in his forties and "valetudinaire" (p. 36), i.e. in poor health. Poussin's excitement at visiting him proves that he has an astonishing reputation in the art world. He is a great artist: Frenhofer explains that only those "initiated into the innermost secrets of art" (p. 47) can discern the flaws in his painting *Mary the Egyptian*.

However, he does not reach Frenhofer's level, because he does not know the secret of how to give a spark of life to his works. Like Poussin, he would like to see the painting that Frenhofer praises so much, and thus improve as an artist. For him, art is above all else everlasting: "The fruits of love pass quickly, those of art are immortal." (p. 71).

KEYS TO READING

A TWO-FACETED STORY

The short story is a shifting literary genre, whose definition has evolved over time. However, specialists agree on several points, summarised in a note by Baudelaire (French writer and literary critic, 1821-1867): "[the short story] has this immense advantage over the novel of vast proportions, that its brevity adds to the intensity of the effect" (DION R., "Nouvelle" in ARON P., SAINT-JACQUES D. & VIALA A. (eds.), *Le dictionnaire du littéraire*, Paris, Presses universitaires de France, 2002, p. 402). Thus, the short story is characterised by its length – short – and its tight plot leading to a surprising fall. To these two characteristics, we can add the temporal proximity of the events told. Indeed, the novella claims to deliver a true and recent fact to the eyes of the reader.

As a 19th-century author, Balzac is part of a short story vein which, in competition with the reportage and the news item, "uses plausible enunciative settings, on which both fantasy and realism are based" (*ibid.*). Indeed, *The Unknown Masterpiece does* combine these two literary genres.

The Fantastic

In *The Unknown Masterpiece*, the reader is immediately plunged into a fantastical atmosphere, particularly through the character of Frenhofer. Poussin perceives "something diabolical" in him at first sight (p. 34). His description reveals the singularity of this mysterious character "to whom the day [...] lent [...] a fantastic colour" (p. 36). He even appears to be possessed, as soon as he has brushes in his hands: "it seemed as if there was a demon in the body of this strange character who acted through his hands, taking them fantastically against the will of the man." (p. 49).

The supernatural thus seems to emerge from the real, especially since Poussin's statements are hesitant, as if he were unsure of the reality of what he sees of Frenhofer. It should also be noted that while Porbus and Poussin existed, Frenhofer is the only painter to be fictional. This invention increases the fantastic aura of the character, who becomes a kind of ghost in a plausible and realistic story.

The mystery surrounding the masterpiece, *La Belle Noiseuse*, further enhances the fantastic and mysterious atmosphere of the story. The painter describes this work as the equal of a woman with the breath of life. He jealously guards it for himself. The reader is left wondering why the painter's studio and his masterpiece are such a secret: What can it contain? What is this perfect work? Does it really exist? All these questions are only resolved in the final pages of the story, in which the madness of the creator is revealed to us.

Realism

Apart from the fantastical touches, the story is rooted in reality. The story is quite plausible regarding, among other things:

- **The descriptions**. From the very first lines, Balzac describes in detail the places, clothes and people Poussin meets. For example, Porbus's studio is described in detail. The reader discovers a host of details and, among other things, that "[n]umerous sketches, studies in three pencils, red chalk or pen, covered the walls to the ceiling. Boxes of colours, bottles of oil and petrol, and overturned steps left only a narrow path to the halo projected by the high glass roof" (p. 37). He can now picture every place, every detail of the setting. In addition to the enumerations and the precision of the vocabulary, there is an abundance of adjectives which also contribute to the realism of the descriptions: "Imagine a bald, bulging, prominent forehead, falling back over a small, crushed nose, turned up at the tip like that of Rabelais [French writer, ca. 1494-1553] or Socrates [Greek philosopher, 470 BC-399 BC]." (p. 34);

- **Places and events**. Occasionally, street names are given. The reader can thus visualise the setting in which the characters evolve. They go from Porbus's house "situated in the rue des Grands-Augustins, in Paris" (p. 32) to "[Frenhofer's] beautiful wooden house near the Pont Saint-Michel" (p. 50), and Poussin goes "to the rue de la Harpe [and] the modest hostelry where he was staying" (p. 60). Thus, the reader can follow the footsteps of the characters in the 6th arrondissement of Paris, close to Notre-Dame Cathedral. In addition, several allusions to historical events are made. Indeed, the year 1612, during which the story takes place, is a "time of turmoil and revolutions" (p. 38). France had just emerged from a long period of civil war, with the Wars of Religion raging for almost 36 years. This almost endless succession of wars between Catholics and Protestants turned the country upside down. The wars officially ended with the signing of the Edict of Nantes in 1598. Yet Frenhofer surprises his guests with "smoked ham [and] good wine [...] despite the bad times" (p. 50). The wars also undermined royal authority, destabilising the country and its organisation. King Henry IV was assassinated in 1610, two years before the story at hand;

- **The real characters**. Two of the three main characters are famous 17th-century painters, Porbus (Frans Pourbus the Younger) and Nicolas Poussin. Moreover, in *The Unknown Masterpiece there* are numerous references to great names in painting: from Mabuse to Giorgione, Raphael (Italian painter and architect, 1483-1520), Rubens, or Rembrandt (Dutch painter and engraver, 1606-1669), the text is full of these illustrious references. Beyond the simple evocation, Balzac offers the reader a discourse on pictorial art, a kind of commentary on the history of art. Frenhofer thus places himself as a spokesman and theorist of painting, particularly when he discusses the work of Porbus: "You floated undecided between the two systems, between drawing and colour, between the meticulous phlegm, the precise stiffness of the old German masters and the dazzling ardour, the happy abundance of the Italian painters." (p. 41). The discourse on painting goes even further by addressing the theme of the artist seen as a creator, not "a vile copyist" (p. 42).

For these and other reasons, this novella is close to a sub-genre of novels, the so-called 'painter's novel'. This sub-genre falls into the category of the biographical novel as well as the historical novel. It is a type of novel that emerged in the 19th century and focuses on the issues of painting. The plot revolves around a painter's character or a painting project. Examples include *L'OEuvre* by Zola (French writer, 1840-1902) or *Manette Salomon* by the Goncourt brothers (French writers Edmond [1822-1896] and Jules [1830-1870]). The dialogue between painting and literature was open during this period and often led to collaborations.

For example, one of the most famous collaborations was the friendly relationship between Claude Monet (French painter, 1840-1926) and Stéphane Mallarmé (French poet and critic, 1842-1898). The two men exchanged views on art and became partners, for example when Monet illustrated Mallarmé's translation of *The Raven* by Edgar Allan Poe (American writer, 1809-1849). In addition to this, many other collaborations took place in the salons where writers, painters, musicians, and other intellectuals met.

A ROMANTIC CONCEPTION OF ART

Although the plot is set in the early 17th century, Balzac's short story nevertheless presents a vision of art and the artist that is specific to his time:

- **Painters by vocation**. The three protagonists are painters by vocation. They live for art, which they see as a pure, almost religious activity. Being a painter is part of their identity. Poussin's deepest desire is to pursue a great career as an artist, for which he feels destined. Frenhofer, on the other hand, embodies the artist of genius in the sense that he does not merely copy the aesthetic canons, but creates something new. This profile of the artist did not appear until the 19th century. In the 17th century, art was considered a form of craft, a trade;

- **Poverty**. The poverty in which Poussin lives echoes the bohemian artists' circles of the 19th century who claimed their poverty in opposition to the values of the bourgeois class;

- **Innate talent**. To become a great artist, one must undergo the magic of initiation. In his short story, Balzac rejects the idea of a long apprenticeship, which was nevertheless de rigueur in the 1600s. Poussin has no intention of going to an art school: he is already talented, but he wants to be initiated by Frenhofer into the secrets of art;

- **The studio**. The studio is a private place where the painter creates alone. In the 17th century, however, most studios were collective places.

These are all characteristics of the Romantic movement.

 ROMANTICISM AND ITS HEROES

The Romantic movement took shape at the end of the 18th century in various European countries, starting with Germany and England. Joined by France, the movement brought together writers and artists who rejected the rationalism of the Enlightenment. These writers and artists wanted to emphasise the exploration of the passions of the self and communion with nature, full of riches and secrets. From then on, Classical order and rules were rejected in favour of creative freedom.

While the movement developed gradually around 1800, the use of the word "Romanticism" to designate the literary and cultural movement dates from 1820. In France, the year 1830 saw the establishment of Romanticism following the Battle of Hernani. This founding event was the public presentation of a theatrical drama by Victor Hugo (French writer, 1802-1885). During the performance, the Classics, judging the play to be revolutionary and disrespectful, heckled and whistled. The Romantics, on the other hand, supported it.

The Romantic movement is not homogenous, but the artists claiming to be part of it agree on a few major principles, such as the desire to break free from classical shackles and the expression of emotion and lyricism *through* authentic speech. The Romantics also wanted to mix genres and registers. Thus, artists were interested in all art forms: writers and painters worked together, as did poets and musicians.

In addition, the authors place romantic heroes at the heart of their plots, who are sensitive and passionate beings with an often thwarted, even tragic destiny. They often come up against society, which denies their aspirations. Divided between hope and disenchantment, they shut themselves away in their solitude, their isolation and, sometimes, their art. Romantic artists also emphasised inspiration, creativity, and innate talent over hard work.

SIGNIFICANT MYTHOLOGICAL REFERENCES

The story includes several references to ancient myths (e.g. to Proteus, a god capable of metamorphosis, or to Orpheus, the poet who descends to the Underworld to save his wife) or to biblical stories (through the evocation of the painting *Mary the Egyptian* by Porbus or of Mabuse's *Adam and Eve* [ca. 1525]).

The author also cites two mythical heroes that are directly relevant to Frenhofer's situation:

- On the one hand, Prometheus, the god who created man out of clay and gave him fire. Like Prometheus, Frenhofer adopts the posture of creator of a living being. Both are punished for their actions: Prometheus is condemned to have his liver eaten for eternity by an eagle, while Frenhofer commits suicide;

- On the other hand, Pygmalion, a sculptor in love with one of his creations, Galatea. Like this artist, the Balzacian painter is in love with his creation, with his Catherine Lescault.

These mythological references enrich the character: they give him a higher dimension. Frenhofer thus becomes more than just a man. For Poussin, he is the "god of painting" (p. 53); Balzac's text explicitly conveys this idea:

> *"This white-eyed, attentive and stupid old man, who had become more than a man to him, appeared to him as a whimsical genius who lived in an unknown sphere. [Everything about this old man went beyond the bounds of human nature. What Nicolas Poussin's rich imagination could grasp clearly and perceptibly when he saw this supernatural being was a complete image of the artist's nature, of that mad nature to which so many powers are entrusted" (p. 57).*

THE QUESTION OF *MIMESIS*

The question of whether art faithfully reproduces reality has been raised since antiquity. The judgements made about the notion of *mimesis* (Greek for 'imitation', 'representation') are varied. *The Unknown Masterpiece* can be seen as a new position in this age-old discussion. The author creates a character who believes that a perfect painting goes beyond the mere representation of the world: for Frenhofer, the painter must paint figures that give the impression that they can be touched or felt, just like real objects.

His criticism of Porbus's paintings revolves precisely around that spark of life with which paintings must be endowed if they are to achieve the status of master-pieces. According to Frenhofer, painting and reality must merge. It is interesting to note that in the novella this relationship goes both ways, as reality can also give the illusion of being a pictorial representation. This is the impression Poussin gets when he first sees Frenhofer: "You looked like a Rembrandt painting walking silently and unframed in the black atmosphere that this great painter has appropriated." (p. 36).

The denouement of the story seems to proclaim the failure of *mimesis*: the character, who wanted to push the logic of imitating nature to the end, does not succeed in realising his ambitions. Art has its limits and one must know how to accept them.

A LEGACY IN THE ARTS

With *The Unknown Masterpiece*, Balzac places himself as a visionary. He develops not just a discourse on painting, but his own reflection on the arts taken as a whole. Written in a period of cultural and literary upheaval, Balzac's novella itself seems to be in the pictorial avant-garde, particularly through the drama of Frenhofer's failure of *mimesis*. This drama evolves into a new conception of art that will only be realised a century later: abstract art.

Abstract art is an artistic movement of the 20th century that includes several very diverse movements. The common characteristic of these different movements is that, unlike figurative art, they evoke feelings and sensations through shapes and colours, without trying to represent reality.

Thus, Frenhofer's painting, as described in the novella, seems to be an abstract, symbolic, non-figurative painting. In this account, Balzac seems to be proposing the culmination of a century-long cultural and pictorial reflection. Indeed, this avant-garde reflection shows us that the perfect representation sought by the 19th century realists is impossible. This is why Frenhofer's painting inevitably inspired the following artists.

The story has therefore had a certain posterity in the arts. Indeed, several painters were inspired by the story in their paintings. Some, like Cézanne (French painter, 1839-1906), even recognised themselves in the features of the disillusioned master whose masterpiece was not recognised by his contemporaries. In fact, Cézanne produced *The Painter Frenhofer Guarding his Unknown Masterpiece* and *Frenhofer Shows his Masterpiece* around 1867-1872.

The aura of the fictional painter and his masterpiece was reflected in many paintings:

- *Madame Kupka among the verticals* (1910-1911) by Kupka (Czech painter, draughtsman and printmaker, 1871-1957);

- The different versions (between 1914 and 1964) of *The Painter and his Model* by Picasso (Spanish painter, engraver and sculptor, 1881-1973);

- *Woman I* (1950-1952) by De Kooning (Dutch painter, 1904-1997);

- *La Demi-sœur de l'inconnue* (1961) by Dufrêne (French painter, 1930-1982);

- *The Unknown Masterpiece* (1982) by Kiefer (German painter, born 1945).

All these painters seem to have been inspired by Frenhofer's work, which appears to be a kind of avant-garde of the impressionist, expressionist and surrealist movements. The art of the master Frenhofer, the fruit of Balzac's imagination, thus appears to be a premonitory dream.

AVENUES FOR FEFLECTION

A FEW QUESTIONS FOR FURTHER REFLECTION...

- Why do you think Balzac introduced painters who really existed into his story?

- Poussin is torn between two feelings; explain which and why.

- The dialogue between painting and literature has been open and fruitful since the 19th century. How is *The Unknown Masterpiece* a good example? Think of the author, Balzac.

- Could Poussin and Porbus be considered responsible for Frenhofer's death? Justify this.

- Does Balzac give an accurate account of the condition of the painter in the 17th century? Develop your thoughts with the help of specific examples.

- In a letter to Madame Hanska (Polish noblewoman, 1801-1882) of 24 May 1837, Balzac states that "the work and the execution [are] killed by the too great abundance of the creative principle". Show how this rule is present both in *The Unknown Masterpiece* and in two other short stories in his *Philosophical Studies*, *Gambara* and *Massimilla Doni*.

- Compare the figure of the painter in *The Unknown Masterpiece* with the one in Zola's *The Work*.

- Can Frenhofer's painting be seen as a precursor of the abstract art that emerged in the 20th century?

- The short story has had a certain posterity in the arts. What aspects of the short story have influenced these painters?

- What are the significant changes in Jacques Rivette's (French filmmaker, 1928-2016) film adaptation of *La Belle Noiseuse* compared to the novella? What can justify them?

TO GO FURTHER

REFERENCE EDITION

DE BALZAC H., *Le Chef-d'œuvre inconnu* suivi de *La Leçon de violon*, Paris, Le Livre de Poche, coll. « Les classiques d'aujourd'hui », 2002.

BASELINE STUDY

ARON P., SAINT-JACQUES D. and VIALA A. (dir.), *Le dictionnaire du littéraire*, Paris, Presses universitaires de France, 2002.

DE BALZAC H., *OEuvres complètes*, tome I, Paris, Alexandre Houssiaux, 1855.

PAILLARD M.-C. (ed.), *Le roman du peintre*, Clermont-Ferrand, Presses universitaires Blaise Pascal, 2008.

ADAPTATION

La Belle Noiseuse, film by Jacques Rivette, with Michel Piccoli, Emmanuelle Béart, Jane Birkin and David Bursztein, France, 1991.

Your opinion is important to us!
Leave a comment on the website of your online bookshop
and share your favourites on social networks!

www.brightsummaries.com

Ebook EAN: 9782808686648
Paperback EAN: 9782808698047
Legal Deposit: D/2023/12603/1084

Cover: © Primento
Digital conception by Primento, the digital partner of publishers.